The Age of the Rainmakers

by the same author

*

The
Age of the Rainmakers

WILSON HARRIS

Illustrated by
Karen Usborne

FABER AND FABER
3 Queen Square, London

First published in 1971
by Faber and Faber Limited
3 Queen Square London WC1
Printed in Great Britain by
Latimer Trend & Co Ltd Plymouth
All rights reserved

ISBN 0 571 09463 5

For MARGARET and TONY
and to the memory of JAMES GLASFORD

The author wishes to thank the Arts Council for financial assistance during the writing of this book and of its preceding companion volume *The Sleepers of Roraima*.

Originality is the fragile yet indestructible arch of community whose web is akin to but other than space.

RAINMAKER'S EPITAPH

Contents

The Age of Kaie

NOTE

The twins of rain and drought—as certain vestiges of Macusi legend imply—are instinctive to the symbolism of the Guianas and Brazil—to great spirit Makonaima and great ancestor Kaie.

I have attempted in this story to interpret the rainmaking fabric of the Macusis as a conception of opposites which has largely been obliterated by histories of conquest—Carib, Spanish, French, English, etc.

Paterson, the half-caste twentieth-century revolutionary, becomes—in this fable—an intimate extension of ancestor Kaie in a long line of guerrilla camouflage—stone-flower of the conquistador. Young Kaie is mortally wounded fighting beside him.

The broken fabric of Macusi legend conceals its true scale —in relating animal features to the gods—and may never have possessed, from the very beginning, an exclusive sum of visual characteristics.

A musical dialogue in nature may be closer to the mysterious ruin of hunter and hunted which is all we possess now like a ballet of the species, and this brings into a different and subtler focus the reeling dance of the dreaded bat of Makonaima—to take one peculiar example—whose fantastic ultrasonic rapport with creatures on land and under water, as it flies through the air, has begun to occupy the mind of art and science as complex iconography akin to a genuine opus or spectre of need whatever assumptions of diabolical appetite are associated with it.

I have attempted in this fable—through an accumulation of particulars bordering upon self-revelation/self-deception—to draw as close as I can to the sacrificial momentum of Kaieteur Fall as icon or caveat wherein ancestor Kaie, in concert with Makonaima's self-generating brood of elements (tree, animal, etc.), broke the drought overshadowing his people.

The Age of Kaie may be read as a story in its own right but it gains in focus, I believe, when reconsidered as part of the entire context of The Age of the Rainmakers. For it is related to a certain drama of consciousness incorporating compensatory roles of the evaporation as well as precipitation of the spirits of the tribe.

Each successive story in this volume looks back to The Age of Kaie in some particular way that may enhance a certain train of associations and Arawak Horizon, the last story, serves to condense an overlap between the absence and presence of gods in history through ironical furnitures or economic omens.

One

Roraima and Kaieteur are the fabric of a curious gateway into South America north of and almost parallel
to the dust of the Equator: drenched in sleep and cloud
—shot through again by imminent distances like float-
ing unruly perspectives in the wake of an expedition.

"Gateway of legend," Paterson said to Kaie, the
young Macusi warrior who lay dying at his side, "and
though it appears sometimes easy to enter, at other
times—even when one's inside—it feels shut in one's
face like mathematics of cloud and sky. Or if not shut,"
he added wryly, "full of pitfalls and contours as though
subject to dreaming ores (inside/out, outside/in) which
swing the needle of one's compass from pole to pole.
What a jump, Kaie," and he laughed. "Perhaps we do
it all the time without knowing. We jump. . . ." He
caught his breath sharply as the pain stabbed. "Jump
where and with what?" asked Kaie.

"With the pole of the elements into other creatures
and ages, magnetic pasts and futures." He laughed
chokingly and shrugged half at himself, half at Kaie;
then with an effort lifted himself on an elbow which

grew now beneath him into something more than the mere stump of fate; shook his wrist like a compass; lifted two fingers to eye, took aim and bearing on the game of space far across the plateau—sky of the mountains. As he held the hallucinated compass and discerned a whirl of numbers, exploding stars, he could hear again—as if it were all happening at this very moment—a burst of fire from the direction of the waterfall.

The rain began to fall but on second thoughts he said to Kaie—"Not rain—blood." Then he remembered: the torn waterfall of creation pounding on the rocks like mute cannon of an archaic legend sometimes blew its echo or spray (they seemed indistinguishable) far across the land—paint of the sun raining a mythical aspect of landscape which sometimes rose into the wounded guardian of the gate. It was here on this very ground that government troops had appeared and fired with eccentric guns—machines of space—at a parcel of rebellious primitives, Paterson's Indians. Paterson saw them as a parcel—his poor guerrilla bands of time—because as they fled a large sheet of paper wrapped around him, half-vapour, half-cloud, split down the middle and they tumbled out of his side. Tumbled out of his paper into the epitaph of space.

Kaie and Paterson had been hit, others killed outright as the party scattered. Loss of blood gave them (Paterson and Kaie) this sensation of paper and space as if they shared the same interior, the same echoing body of fragmentary particulars, and the elements were hallucinated within them and without.

Kaie was aware that Paterson was elated, common-or-garden camouflage, god's paper of space: the *naïveté* of revolutionary fatherhood. The others, he knew, who escaped unhurt, had scattered—in keeping with previous instructions—in twos and threes—some up to the mountains to blend, as it were, into a mosaic of cloud; some into Brazilian rivers to blend, as it were, into a mosaic of water; some into caves to blend, as it were, into a mosaic of rock.

Through a fringe of bush where they lay on the ground they dreamt they could reach out and touch the mountains. If they could gain those, Kaie felt, they would be safe for a while but how could they make it when enemy troops were patrolling. . . .

"Might as well walk in air, in space," Paterson said and fell back with a sense of drought. It began to dawn on him in his broken frame of mind—fertile resemblances (Indian tree, sky, water, rock) fathered by drought—that the parent of revolution was itself the offspring of deficiency which he (Paterson) had witnessed in the paint of the sun like food of memory.

Was this debilitation of premises (blood-bank of space) an extension of the death of the gods into the fabric of revolution?

"Our enemies", said Paterson hypnotically as he lay dying, "are *our* fierce nostalgic creation, *our* hope of compensation, *our* hope of heaven or hell. We who are weak create what is strong. We bend our last gasp to the creation of the enemy—as our own guard—patrol of immortality. . . ."

His voice rose and fell with hollow flippancy—

hollow self-mockery—to which suddenly there came
an answering cry like a long-dead echo, ancestor Kaie
—cat or bird mewing to the conquistador of heaven.
And Paterson had the curious ironic sensation that in
the hollow pit of his body—ancestral Indian enemy—
Kaie's breath had been caged for centuries instinctive to
the residue of legend—betrothal of opposites. Kaie felt
now as if he were looking through Paterson across the
long drought of an age within which the dust of initiation rippled again and swirled again upon a canvas familiar with ruin, endless marches, counter-marches, patrols.

Often in the past they had lain like this side by side—
drunk with the glory of hope akin to despair like
soldiers on a spree—a giant spree—*Drink Deep—Drink
Death*. Kaie choked as if the dust were settling in his
throat, choked as Paterson laughed and clapped him on
the back.

"A great drought," Paterson confessed, "when your
namesake or ancestor was taken prisoner. He was called
king of the house of betrothal—of the hollow maiden
of the tribe." He laughed still as he clapped Kaie on the
back. Then suddenly as if to push him *there*—back into
the past—archaic skeleton—he cried, "Quick. Lie still,
the patrol's coming." Kaie fell flat on mother earth and
kissed the ground as if it were the bride of the gods. He
could hear the tramp of the patrol going past perhaps
twenty feet away. It was curious but as they passed the
thick drapery of the bush established an illusion of
distance (as if twenty paces were a thousand years or as
if each echoing boot pushed him down into the cradle
or the grave).

"It's true," said Paterson and whistled the bird-song of the Macusis under his breath. "The distances of history melt or multiply with each convertible echo." Kaie nodded lifting his eyes now to the colour of the sun which seemed to clothe the skeleton of history with a diffused radiance or waterfall of leaves; as the sounding step of the patrol faded the echo of his breath, caged in Paterson, died in unison with it and Kaie dreamt—as his senses ebbed and flowed—that he stood within a great hollow body scooped from the guerrilla of ages into a new maiden architecture of place. Scooped and dispersed at the same time into a savage/tender carpet painted with a waterfall of seasons—suns, moons, days, nights—upon which every young warrior of the tribe, from the beginning of ancestors, slept with the maiden of his choice ringed closely by a patrolling design of the enemy whose fists were her breasts, taut and green and poised.

Within that maiden architecture—house of betrothal —a single star shone, as night began to fall, against which loomed, at first faint then clearer by degrees, the shadow of the enemy scout and Kaie saw, with his heart in his mouth, that a single member of the cunning ring on patrol had returned across the plateau and noiselessly bore down on him. Without a word they grappled—heartbeat of the enemy—initiation of love —the beginning of a long secret corridor within the hollow maiden of the tribe (stone-flower of the conquistador) which would lead—if all went well— through darknesses like conflagrations to the treaty of the sun.

21

Her breasts, the enemy's fists, sent him reeling but they closed again and this time he stabbed. The enemy crumpled and Kaie sank to his knees with the sense that he had unwittingly reopened a wound, an ancient wound it seemed he remembered receiving himself a long, long time ago. . . . He began to clean the blade of his knife until the friction of cloth on metal—like flesh in stone—became as subtle as the ruin of life, dead scout, endless bride.

2

It was this subtle voice coming it seemed from the bride of the forest which attuned him to the renewal of mortal danger. He ceased wiping the blade of his knife but the grating sound addressed him still—a whisper of cork drawn around the rim of the world, glass of earth. *Someone was coming.* It had an instantaneous effect. His senses reeled like a moth to a tune—baton of Makonaima.

The star on the carpet in the house of betrothal vanished and a misty half-moon, half-wing steeped everything. At any moment, Kaie knew, the next dreaded scout might loom larger and darker than his predecessor.

There was a drought over the land and the winesoaked cork of the jungle reflected a mirage or feast—spectre of famine—a decline in the volume of the river threading its way on the thinnest wire of sound.

It seemed incongruous and yet fitting that the blade with which he had killed one man had now been re-

fined on its loom into a single wire or thread intimating
the dress of all things: the dress of trees like fantastic-
looking boulders in waterfall or river: the dress of
famine like an unsealed bottle in the hollow of his ribs,
her ribs, too, the maiden of the tribe. It filled him with
rage and tenderness, foreboding and terror as he waited
for the thread of glass to unwind itself afresh—vine,
snake or creeper, claw or bat of the moon.

Kaie saw it closing in on him; he thrust the dead
scout in his side towards the claw of the patrol, half-
wing of darkness, half-hood of light. And the bat or
patrol which flew towards him suddenly stopped in
its tracks, conscious all of a sudden that its own blood
had been spilled, its own familiar ruin or face; it
hovered there for an instant as if the threads of love and
death, flesh and spirit had crossed: then deciding swiftly
to leave Kaie alone and take the other tangible reflection, caught the dripping bottle he had flung—
caught it securely as Kaie caught her, the hollow tribe
of his soul. As it withdrew with the dregs from the
bottle on its lips, it sealed a kiss, betrothal of opposites,
wine of the feast, mirage, celebration, thread of famine,
thread of reality, thread of cosmos: sealed it within a
capacity to unravel its own patrol of subsistence, its
own remorseless self-consumption, appetite for fear,
doom, revolution, echo of solipsis.

The house of betrothal—ground of Makonaima—
stretched from an inconspicuous seed to an inconspicuous sound—birth of lightning to seal of thunder.
The tree of rain grew to enfold it (that house of the

maiden) and the women of the Macusis dreamt they could measure the sum of its parts by relating Kaie (man-seed) to a flower or guardian at their gate; others to a drought or jealous god at their gate.

They brought their separate vessels, therefore, to the door of the hollow maiden of the tribe with whom Kaie slept.

Slept, as it were, with the ear of his heart to the shell of the ground—inconspicuous seed to inconspicuous sound. He could hear the feet of the vessels—ring of feminine mould—where before there had been a concert of masculine stones—enemy patrol. As though in some curious way each ancient stone guarding the gate to the house of betrothal was unsealed now—unstoppered now into a pact between mass and hollow, flesh and spirit, nature and psyche—extending over the centuries like the architecture of a new age compounding love and war—violence and fate—into the *caveat* of form. With the death of Paterson (half-caste modern revolutionary) it was as if a long-standing drought issuing from the very patriarch of guerrillas—stone-flower of the conquistador—became the anatomy of conquest unsealed now as the new feminine guardian of the gate darkening in a flash into a gigantic rose or waterfall descending towards them—hollow maiden of the tribe with whom Kaie slept in a rainmaking betrothal fashioned from need—their need to reconcile the twin elements. He could hear the fall of each petal as it settled into the patrol of the centuries carven from the stone-flower of the conquistador. On his first encounter with the twin shadow of the enemy he had been smitten by drought fists, green breasts; on his second encounter he had thrust the shadow of death from him, the echo of solipsis; now it was the anatomy of lightning fury guarding his gate in the name of conquest which began to assault him like an accumulation of tyrannies associated with the hollow deeds of man encircled by the arms of woman. . . .

He dreamt he moved in secret file down the brow of a pass, throat, lips of the conquistador—ambush or maiden. When the stroke fell they drew together, man to man, Kaie to maiden, like fingers on one hand. Five in all each shod in his separate callous. It rested there— that hand of god—upon its pass of love or death. *Kaie recalled it clearly:* it was his maiden engagement—his first real clash with the enemy in the body of their continent. All previous engagements faded now into mere skirmishes. Here, in the "conquistador pass" as the guerrillas christened it, lay the true maiden—the true baptism—of fire. Late in the afternoon when his own side withdrew he (Kaie) was left behind, presumed dead. He lay beside four others in fanwise formation— heads together like curious lovers kissing the ground, re-creating amongst themselves the subconscious hand of fate that had felled them from above. Kaie made the fifth finger on that hand which extended from a wrist of stone across the landscape and when the enemy patrol descended they, too, were struck by this finger (Kaie's body) crooked or twisted a little on its own shadow or trigger.

As the shadow of the patrol moved on, a bodiless hallucination possessed him—the wounded man. Not

so much bodilessness as extreme isolation in association
with the hand of death, extreme quick of life, extreme
nail or paradox which began to compensate itself within a gigantic guardian of place reaching across the conquistador valley or maiden of earth. Reaching, as it
were, from one ruined side to the other whether victor
or victim, bodiless or bodily. One hand—with its giant
fingers—each tall as a man—rested here on this side of
eternity. The other fell there, on the other side of time,
within his own retreating band of guerrillas who had
stopped and out of exhaustion thrown themselves to
the ground within an identical fanwise formation,
heads together on a wrist of stone, limbs straight out.
Except for one crooked body or finger like Kaie's on
its shadow or trigger.

As he lay thus across the hollow breast of war, as if
it were the maiden of the cosmos, he felt himself in-
wardly wrestling with the hallucinated ambivalence of
one flesh extending from nail into knuckle into wrist
into shoulder into death into life with such abruptness
and precariousness he feared it might materialize too
swiftly and cave in, as a consequence, into intimate
boulders on a hill racing, all of a sudden, to the bottom
of the maiden, heart of the valley.

This ambivalent fabric reflected some of the de-
fections, treacheries, treaties, etc. wherein the conquistador pass had changed hands frequently; and yet despite
it all (or because of it all) had acquired a savage mood
of tenderness with each fall-out, each effort to hold or
underpin the pass; so that those who departed and those
who came—as within a sieve of nature—became in-

creasingly involved in a universal spectre or solipsistic deed—boulders of war—the lightning friction of space.

A matchstick flared at this instant quick as the trigger of god across the valley like dust prickling the air to validate the drought of man within the compass of history. A sudden and prolonged thunderburst followed and Kaie saw—when it was over—that an inch of rain had fallen to scale the knuckle of the living/dead finger on the guardian of the gate.

It was late afternoon and the long shadow of that split finger—wound or psyche of the tribe—crept up the walls or fabric of the valley into antlers of metamorphosis upon the head of a bull. As Kaie reached up to grapple across space with these ridges of the conquistador, antlers of memory, antlers of patrol—he was aware of the endless tree of Makonaima (tree of the tribe) that enfolded all places and things within an iconic house of betrothal. A tree whose horns or branches seemed, on one hand, to have preserved everything intact—like the father of self-deception—in close rapport, however, with a tree whose horns of solipsis appeared to have been chopped until a matchless concert grew between mass and hollow, self-revelation, self-deception, father/mother, horned bull/hornless maiden, horned/hornless tree ... *waterfall.* ...

Two

‏❦‎

The rain began to grow upon that hollow tree until a spectre of flood arose and the house of betrothal rocked and shuddered like a boat dragging its anchor towards a waterfall.

Kaie was filled with curious alarm. The conversion of the tree into an impending waterfall—the conversion of the house into a sacrificial boat—seemed, at first, another ruse of the enemy whose patrol he had outwitted before —rain-bottle of Makonaima, dead scout, green maiden, drought fists, quick of life, fan of memory.

But then as the chain of associations which hampered the boat, even as it released the house, ran through his hands like a ghost Kaie was aware of two anchors—not one—he had himself pulled up over the side of his vessel as it began to lift.

Two anchors—one grey, one green—lodged together. His namesake ghost, long-dead ancestor, had sown the grey one as the spectre of the flood; he, Kaie, scion of memory, had sown the green one as the bait of the flood. And one had caught the other: two ages intertwined: anchor-in-anchor, bait-in-spectre.

It was an ironic catch for as it struck the deck, arm-in-arm, bait-in-spectre, its crooked fingers arose like rescuer and rescued in the tree of the waterfall which spread now and branched in all directions.

It gave Kaie the lightning almost hilarious sensation that he had himself dived in and pulled Paterson up—in the nick of time—from the grey cloak of ancestral death which swirled around Makonaima's shoulders threaded at the same time with a sobering counterpoint—scales, knuckles—like a curious almost clerical claw, ambassadorial animal, animal of god.

On the other hand Kaie wondered whether it was he who had been rescued from green bottled depths—spectral primitive blood: swift claw, hollow revolutionary/sacrificial proportions—self-deception, self-initiation, self-absorption of deeds—which drew him back to surface across the ages within a blithe uncanny mirror antlered with grey as well as green stumps of affection.

That these stumps, which stood now on the deck of betrothal, were the hand of the god of the waterfall—the enduring spark and *caveat* of the rainmaker, anchor lodged in anchor, fist in fist, finger kissing finger—may have seemed incongruous and barren to Kaie a day or two ago, an hour or two ago, a minute or two ago but *now*, as his senses dived and returned within an associated comedy of the elements, he felt himself addressed by the ambassador of rain.

"My credentials," said the ambassador presenting his anchors.

"They look", said Kaie, "as if they've come from the

bottom of the sea. Is that where your country lies—the dead of the sea?"

"Dead of the sea—yes," said the ambassador half-reflectively, half-ruefully. "That's one finger." He lifted his grey-green stumpy hand and shook it half-mockingly, half-seriously, "Here's another—dead of land. And another—dead of day. And another—dead of night. Lastly—dead of the waterfall. Five fingers in all. Do you remember now?"

Kaie was astonished. "How can you encompass . . .?" he began.

"I encompass *you*", said the ambassador, "on the stumps of the rain-god."

"Compass, compass," cried Paterson all of a sudden like a child stumbling in the dark, stuttering in the dark, as he sought to lift two fingers on that living/dead hand of the ambassador—two fingers like the sights of a gun across the plateau, exploding stars.

"Forked finger," said Kaie, stumbling too, stuttering too where his body arched on its lightning shadow or trigger—hand of the globe.

"Five fingers in all," said the ambassador of the rain-god raising aloft the fabric of sky and earth.

"Why do you call yourself *dead of the sea*?" asked Kaie addressing the first stump or finger on that grey-green twin anchor.

"Ah," said the stump shod in his callous, yellow callous, black skin, grey age, green youth, "I am the ring of the land around the sea: the scale of the rain, the hollow knuckle. I am the middle passage of the waterfall. See how it pours like a ghost in chains. Anchor of a slave." As the stump spoke the tree rose higher still towards its waterfall, climax, memorial.

"And why do you call yourself *dead of the land*?" Kaie spoke now with insistent breath to the second stump on that mimic hand, yellow-black chain, clanking ghost.

"Ah," said the ghost unshackling his chain, "I am the cup of the sea, the quick of the rain, dice of song. I lead the chorus of the waterfall—seedtime, harvest-time, drought-time, floodtime. Can you hear me . . .?"

The tree rose again, gigantic rose, hollow maiden of the waterfall whose gamble with life and death Kaie heard now—as if for the first time—like seed rattling in a cup, maiden of space.

The ambassador shook that cup and as the dice rained in the waterfall Kaie could see one eye on one face, two eyes on another, three, four, five, six which sped like cubes of cloud, wager of harvest, *die of sea, die* of *land*.

But Kaie was still not satisfied with the wager of the fall and he addressed himself afresh to the confusing hand of the ambassador—"One more question, ambassador—why do you call yourself *dead of day*?" His breath caught in his throat like a relentless fury.

"Coffin of rain," said the ambassador with a curious self-mocking smile. "You threw it at me, remember? I caught it. . . ." He opened his claw and revealed the die of slavery cast upon every trail into every dangerous occupation of the future, occupation of natures, old orders, new guerrillas.

Kaie was astonished and incredulous—smitten by archaic delirium or siege, cube of the waterfall—"Shall

31

I lie with you forever in the same black coffin?" he cried half-forgetting, half-caste revolutionary, "the same white coffin?" He paused to stroke the air—"Or do I die now in truth to resuscitate you out of fear, scout of the underworld, to throw you back my own glasshouse of necessity, lost mountains, lost rivers, lost valleys—to do with as you wish under the same assumed name—black father, black revolution, white father, white revolution, beggarman, beggar-coffin, kingman, king-coffin, son-of-man. . . ."

The rain bowed its head into a torrent of familiars through whose thickets Kaie discerned—it seemed to him now—the self-created author of conquest; and yet something spectral, nevertheless, *incommensurable* with ruin, issued like the dust of betrothal, spirit of the fall, death of the gods, blood of man.

"Large as life now," Kaie shot back, taking advantage of this, material deed, material doggedness, triumphant at the mist of his own blood which scaled Paterson's, cloaked the sky. "I can measure you—pin you down," he cried and choked—cloud of incomprehension. "I can *measure* . . ." choked afresh on a sense of the monstrous deadly wager of freedom—crucifixion of the elements. The tree of his breath ascended like a thread in the waterfall as if to unravel that cloud in the coat of a universal ambassador—ambassador of the *quick* of the rain at dead of day or dead of night.

"Well, that's that," the special correspondent said, closing up his camera. "That last one should be a good shot. Funny the way these five are spread-eagled."

He lit a cigarette. In the distance he could hear the muted thunder of the waterfall punctuated by desultory firing. The last handful of rebels and the government troops fought on.

The Mind of Awakaipu

NOTE

In The Marches Of El Dorado *Michael Swan speaks of the "well-documented" story of Awakaipu with mixed feelings, scepticism and belief, which reflect his own biases. Today it is becoming clearer that the kind of stoical behaviour attributed to the Indians of America north and south may reflect a complex solipsis or wishfulfilment in which explorer and explored have been involved for centuries as part and parcel of the long forlorn adventure of history.*

This solipsis became increasingly dogmatic within an apparent factuality—a partiality to fearful deeds—which overlooks inner perspectives, iconic alternatives.

The story or stories circulated about Awakaipu, the Arekuna Indian, in the nineteenth century are largely bound up I feel (some of my antecedents are Amerindian) with projections of a formal pattern—an unfeeling heroic consensus, closed plot, consolidated function or character—upon the inner breakdown of tribal peoples long subject to conquest and catastrophe.

Swan writes how Richard Schomburgk, the German explorer, "speaks in admiration of the way he (Awakaipu) behaved when attacked by perai—'biting his lips with the raging agony he rolled about in the sand; yet no tears flowed from his eyes, no cry passed his lips'."

Note

This kind of tale—to which has been added a sacrificial massacre performed by Awakaipu to change the skin of his race from brown to white—was common in the nineteenth century (and still is in the twentieth) as the fixed character of an age and it has endorsed the predicament of the Indian throughout the Americas. Swan himself admits that "it is a strange story with no indication of the real state of Awakaipu's mind".

It is a sombre fact that entire peoples can be conscripted within a deed to fashion the aboriginal face of a world because of a formidable hiatus—a loss of imaginative scale—at the heart of primitive realities.

The profound necessity remains therefore to begin to unravel these contradictions within oneself and, by a continuous relativizing process, extend one's horizons beyond the terrifying partiality of an age into a conception of the native as a curious host of consciousness.

This story is another venture in that direction.

Gorge of Awakaipu

I caught my first glimpse of the ruin of a gorge called Awakaipu around noon. The sky was bright and yet in my dream of primitive ancestors the heavens seemed black as in some enormous painting or eclipse of the deed of the sun. When, in fact, Awakaipu himself began to loom in the canvas of that gorge he seemed the constellation not simply of darkness but of curious self-revelation: as though the brushmarks of his cradle of the sun were clearly seen now as a bright callous, a glaring misconception of nature, a blind manner or seizure by light.

I approached him and said to him—"I would like to explore the gorge. . . ."

"Gorge!" his face grew black as if he wished now to run from me into the heart of space. "Awakaipu," I cried. "Awakaipu." I recalled the idea—akin to the gossip of an age—that to name the dead was to hold them ransom to one's will.

He stopped and looked at me with a kind of glimmering self-mockery. Like a snapshot whose ransom of history affected me now equally as it did him. As though both *name* and *will* were tools—economic tools, political tools—to purchase the negative soul of time, his as well as mine.

"What a damnable proposition," I cried. "What a damnable trap."

He looked at me and I knew he agreed.

"It's time to break out, go back ..." I cried, waving towards the heart of the gorge.

I fished in my breastpocket and pulled out a bundle of newspaper clippings entitled *The Deeds of Awakaipu*. They shivered like dry leaves as if in this light they were part and parcel of an inner glow, an ironical furnace. I withdrew one of these and handed it to Awakaipu who gripped it suddenly like a clairvoyant tracing within the object he held—hieroglyphic of night—the ghostly spark of the future. Save that—with Awakaipu—the future evoked the past—one hundred calloused years ago.

"Fire years," said Awakaipu. His eyes were trembling in his mask of sleep.

So slight a tremor, however, I scarcely noticed it and was conscious that in grasping the page of the past his face seemed absolutely set—stylized pattern, ancient colour or leaf, bark of a tree. And yet once again—*there it was*: the faintest tremor quick as a vein of dust across the lid of sleep—dream of the dead, dream of the *deed* of the past as it began to reawaken from nightmare solidarity, nightmare solipsis—to reawaken and hesitantly crumble.

"Dead. Deed," I muttered. "What does it mean?"

I could hear now a sputter coming from his lips, monologue of an obsessed student repeating a lesson a hundred years ago in a laconic, unsettled order. "Code. Behaviour. Never shed a tear."

I began to watch him now as the words crackled on his lips as if coming from afar—century or centuries—to simulate a distant forest fire akin to the invention of the human voice—ancient record—ancient gramophone.

He was reputed—in the first half of the nineteenth century—to be a remarkable Indian pupil. He had learnt to read and write in German and English with a smooth rage and bloodless sophistication far in advance of his time. So much so that few dreamt he nursed a secret lapse into fear and astonishment—a staccato void—when he read an account of himself (and his own native Arekuna customs) by the German botanist and explorer with whom he worked as a guide. He noted, for example, with curious fascination that when bitten by a deadly snake he (Awakaipu)—though subject to pain—had shown implacable indifference, had rolled on the ground without a sound save the chorus of dust—crackle of limbs of earth—and never shed a tear.

"*Never shed a tear.*" As he spoke now I saw that minuscule flicker again on the dreaming mask of indifference—deed frozen upon him.

His tremor now crossed my own lids like the eye of history, reflex of history. "Deed. Dead," I dreamt and flickered as if I were the selfsame pupil, spellbound orb, character of fiction. I saw how driven I was to play in turn at senseless self-persecution, to play a role of uncanny fortitude which bordered on the inhuman, the manner of the inhuman. Never to shed a tear.

As his or my pupil flickered I dreamt the script in Awakaipu's hand was in my hand; I became Awakaipu; returned after a hundred years or more to stand outside of myself—look at myself, the stone ordeal of myself. And thus to impart to the elements something of my own native eclipse or astonishment, in the beginning, when I was cast in Awakaipu's mould.

An eclipse, on one hand, astonishment on the other that a minuscule spark of tenderness had endured to repudiate the strait-jacket of the gods—primitive pattern of hell.

I wondered whether the knowledge that I would return to stand outside of myself in a century or two—an age or two—may not have influenced my consent to entombment within a certain body or colour. Like one who knows at some stage he will inevitably turn and grope backwards into the fetishes and toys of god's childhood which have become synonymous with insensibility encompassing all his descendants on earth to such an alarming violent degree it needs to be exposed as a pathetic gloss upon immortality—upon the multifarious address of inner creative life.

My first impression—as I held the newspaper in my hand—was the manner of illustration (Awakaipu's ornaments) which I wore around my wrists—snake or albatross. A small party—including the German botanist and explorer with whom I worked as a guide—were encamped at Matope. (There are several Matopes in Guiana like a series of calendrical ghosts. For some it is the time of rapids; for others the time of mountains; for others again it is a timeless gorge—an immaterial gorge which exists as a gateway between worlds, between times.)

I rolled on the ground and I could hear now—as my own distant forest fires crackled—the rumble of my employer's voice—mechanical landslide, phonograph.

The snake which bit me, appeared, vanished so swiftly some thought it a bushmaster, others a labaria. It had been, curiously enough, a glancing, frightened, uneasy blow—and the *piaiman* or medicine-man who accompanied the party acted almost contemptuously, extracted fang or poison and applied a cayman's tooth. I rolled on the ground nevertheless in a dead faint—overpowered more by fear than fact—inner roar of blackness, dryness in the throat, rubble of a waterfall, coal or fire, river or slide.

And so where tears rolled down heaven's cheeks before, rocks grew now at the mouth of my gorge into the nuclei of an indifferent cosmos, fortitude, tautology of the primitive, dynastic wasteland, prophetic concentration camp. I saw all this with an inner tremor of the eyelid of the dead, *dead faint*, as I clutched the dry clairvoyant paper in my hand which my employer had used a century and a half ago to press a wild flower, design or occupation of nature.

The medicine-man knelt at my side as I ceased to move and watched the faint landslide, riverslide my employer overlooked. He cupped his hands as if to shelter that flicker or die across the gamble of centuries, seminal dream, seminal tear. So faint that to overlook it was to succumb, all the more merrily, to a blind rage for inventions of historical character, factory of the deed, ordeals, substitutes, tautologies of fire, human chimney stacks as the heart of misconception—drought of tears.

It was thus that the *piaiman* counselled me as though he wished, now that an age was passing, to infiltrate my employer—to be half-employer, half-ironical-medicine priest (capital resources—psychology of the primitive).

And I—standing, as it were, within my own concert of dying/waking times, half-within, half-without the mould of Awakaipu—watched with the *piaiman* the frail lightning of immensity within the head of space he shaped with his hands which I seized upon—in the name of a stoical employer/inventor—as my first initial contradiction, solid lid, shutter of man.

Inscribed on that lid was my first collective deed or seizure of dreams—Matope of the Snake.

Matope of the Snake

Matope of the Snake stands at the entrance to the gorge of Awakaipu. It is a curious headland—sometimes called fist of a piaiman. Clearly it is as if the medicine-man of the tribe had indeed framed a head by cupping his hands together.

When my European employer/explorer first saw it a century and a half ago he was fascinated by this spectacle of character as he christened it.

For this headland/fistland seemed to him the cradle of a people who had banked everything into a composition of purity and greatness.

The stones were so polished they shone with the sun: so great and strong they seemed imbued in their own right with a furnace—omen of eternity.

We had set up camp there—the German botanist, the piaiman, myself and a few others. I was bitten by the half-apologetic snake of god. . . . A glancing blow it was but enough to send me rolling on the ground, fit or faint. I dreamt the colours of earth and water, green botanist and red medicine-man, ran together and I stood, dressed in their variegated emotion, at the entrance to the underworld between the forked fingers of the universe.

I was aware, first of all, that I clung in desperation to those knuckled columns, gateway or gorge. Clung, it seemed, with bliss and courage, clown and demon: clung for a moment or two—an hour or minute in the mind of my employer—which lasted, however, in the flickering dream of the piaiman half-a-century, a full century, a century-and-a-half before it began to crackle like fire, real limbs of fire, decimation of the fires of god.

I dreamt I could read my employer's mask as never before across the thaw of time. Read my own tribal sins as well—sacrificer and sacrificed—monument and victim—thaw of the native host of time.

As the healing thaw flickered on my Awakaipu/ piaiman red eyelid I grew aware of the seminal tears of heaven as the tragic deeds of men which had congealed on the face of the gorge.

As the thaw flickered on my European green eyelid I grew aware of the gorgon of drought as a scale of resources—dewdrop sharp as a diamond—milk frozen into alabaster—shadowplay conscripted into flint.

It was this scale of atonement—red/green eyelid—I read in each seminal tear masked by the wishfulfilment of self-created things, self-created colours.

In my red eyelid had been stored a holocaust of sacrifice—a forest fire which, far back in the calendrical ghosts of creation, swept across the site of the gorge as Matope of the Snake. So swift it doubled and re-doubled in its tracks, glanced this way, writhed that way. Fire-snake of ambition. I could discern it now afresh—that fire-sermon—because as the sun shone on my dead faint it glistened on the rocks with the gleam of ice until an inner thaw parted the world—and drew it together again into new attitudes, apparent totalities, fixations of longing—like an ironical magnet of landscapes, bald crowns or ages, forest spires, rock-ledges. A magnet of time that seemed to lock and unlock the sorrows and wishes of god self-inflicted by men upon men. Stone men painted red. Wood men painted red. Forest men painted red. All—my variegated population—had received that frightened blow, the blow of the fire-snake which assumed such proportions, such executive proportions, it became the *caveat* of murder.

I would have failed to perceive it as my model crime of wishfulfilment had it not been for that ironical *caveat* —seminal thaw—which, in setting up the stoic of ambition, blew from still another quarter the waters of adventure across the face of the gorge.

That water-sermon, water-snake, blew—as the fire-snake had done—round and round, and glanced in all directions as if to re-trace the mirror of unity re-born in its tracks. It was called indeed the river of soul, arose in Matope—and as is the case with many such streamers— wound its way through flags of memory across a loom of retiring fabrics, skeletons, river-beds.

I perceived now that my red eyelid was a seal or invention on the river of the dead. A protective cover I had long misconceived, an umbrella of resources, a dug-out, a trench within the calendrical ghost of earth where-through the fluid elongated tear of god gathered into itself all its mythical robe or harness as sheer host of mankind, initiation of mankind, conception of unity beyond the lapse of places. The unity of long grass or feathered banks of cloud at the heart of the river. The unity of short grass or trimmed lawns of cloud in the hair of the river. The unity of heaven or sky of rapids, reflections, in feather and fin.

I would have failed again to perceive it as an inner community—an inner counsel against the solid yoke of tyranny—had it not been for those seminal rapids which, in escalating the snake of the river, blew from still another quarter across the face of the gorge. This was the landslide of Matope, and—in the beginning—when the gorge of Awakaipu was created, it sped so suddenly it seemed swifter than sermons of fire or water.

So suddenly, so swiftly I would have missed it—that landslide—been buried in it forever—were it not for the voices of fire, sermons of water which still continued far down in the mind of Awakaipu, precipitate races, Adam's races.

I could hear them now like the original accents of fear, misguided fear, thaw of mountains, flawed inventions of pride, land to water to fire.

Races of Matope

A close examination of the face of the gorge of Awa-kaipu reveals the path of the landslide, the path of fire, the path of water as one of the earliest pathological manifestations of races of men. That I began to see it now—to apprehend it now—was a curious omen of the medicine-man as host community: O MEN—circle of man—Awakaipu/Aesculapius. The snake that bit me had bitten its tail far back on the globe with every apparition of conquest—landslide of psychological victory and fear, race between life and death, cure and plague like the lock of god self-imposed by green man upon red. In that premature spring of the elements, bite or fang, snake or deed was conscripted into a fiend or barrier to love.

It was the deed of the race—Adam's tumbling river, Adam's cloven land, Adam's fire—that endorsed a mis-guided fascination with environments of evil, polders, defences between man and man, between creature and creation.

As I began to re-trace it now I was aware of this self-defeating strategy as winding and unwinding neverthe-less into a subconscious thread, circular or otherwise, miraculously flawed, and therefore open to community

like a subtle host of alternatives beyond a collective
fiend. First I found myself on the winding staircase of
the landslide.

There the earth-race lived and moved, gritty,
pebbled, enclosed in the seminal rapids of the landslide,
seminal flood, mask of pity.

Where my red eyelid was stood a red pebble, green
eyelid a green one. I could feel the race of pebbles like a
flurry of marbles in time's hand bouncing down the
staircase of landslide through the sockets of god's childhood until two stuck and held there in my head. Deed of
the eye, monolith of vision. It seemed disconcerting
now that I had been deceived by the sleight-of-hand of a
child—race or game whose flight on the staircase turned
into my frieze or investiture, gorgon's marble, evil eye.
It was deed or monolith I saw again that wrapped my
vision round in the beginning with a conviction of
evil—precipitate seal as the fiend of light.

The pebbles which rained and stuck in their sockets—
in that earth-race—were of infinite susceptibility to my
green and red—black or purple—crimson or pearl—
summer or winter solstice. It was this ceaseless play of
elongated shadow or light that carried the thread of my
vision towards them so subtly, so enormously, it re-
sembled the landslide of the moon—marble of the moon
—the gambol of the tides as an unseen staircase inscribed
minutely nevertheless upon each shell or stone—head or
race—in relation to the sea of day or the stars of night.

It was a combination of the aim of a child and the
frightened target of man that consolidated a misconception of scale—cloven staircase of maturity (half-

child, half-man)—arrested species—half-fable, half-fear
—weather of the gorgon. For as the pebbles raced—as
god's child played its lightning hand at the top of the
landslide—the piaiman bullets he let loose seemed to
glance in all directions (apologetically almost, aimlessly
at times) so that in inscribing their multifarious orient or
compass of origins they seemed to conscript the path of
the stars and the sun into ambivalent fates—a preoccupa-
tion with impersonal spaces, impending densities, punitive raids as well as a conviction of the inefficient sights
of a tyrant, hiatus of storm in whose deed of calm the
earth-race momentarily basked—frozen indifference.

As I peered through that seeming mask of peace,
through that deed of calm that had once smitten me with
such indifference (peered through like one who stood
both within and without his shell of time)—I was aware
of the pathology of eternity (landslide, fireslide, water-
slide) and it seemed to me now that the gorge of Awakaipu (fistland, headland) possessed, in a transition of
ages—for the first revealing time—a self-corrective void
or seminal proportion as the sorrow of freedom; and
the seeming randomness of the piaiman's lightning hand
in that context—finger of the seashore, finger of the
riverbank, finger of valley or ridge—became an intimate web, thaw of space, and universal spectre of care.

SORROW OF FREEDOM

The species of the earth-race—born of the sorrow of
freedom—stood, it seemed, within the self-corrective
void of the staircase I had glimpsed a moment or two

ago and their pebbled apparel drew them together even as it seemed to pull them apart within the piaiman's cup or fist.

I felt I could see them still in their hollow cave as in my own dreaming death shaped by the webbed hand of the medicine-man into elders of landscape—my stunned elders—greybearded children who had aged in their sleep, the deed of sleep. Sleep had, in the beginning, hit them between the eyes as they stood—each in his turn— in heaven which had revolved all of a sudden into the eerie middle or bottom of the staircase, into chopped wave, island page or continental jacket of god. As such their dreams became evil as though the elder of water (the page-child of water) had been turned into a striking mirror or jealous ageing function, and the elder of land (the page-child of land) had been fused into a conniving frame around that jealous ageing function of water mirroring the sun.

For those children or greybeards had been appointed, in turn, as the substitute hand of god to play freely, innocently, with the marble of the sun.

Their appointment occurred before they actually fell though now in tracing their pathological beard—forests of land or water—it was difficult to disentangle when they had been smitten into archaic regions.

Perhaps—in the first place—it was a forest of shadow which the page-child of water mistook for his devilish capture, mirror to palm, wave to land. As such when he fell from the very top of the staircase (from the threshold of heaven) he brought his self-deceptive cloud as the atmosphere of a prison into which he began to age without unshackling himself from mistaken capture, since he wished to preserve a link with the marble of creation he had rolled and imprinted on his hand as the lightning of sleep—god's sleep.

Perhaps—in the second place—it was the lightning in the water against him which the page-child of the land mistook for a devilish firmament. As such when he looked up to the very top of heaven he smote himself in advance—drew himself down in advance—into a captive lifeline or sun. Therefore he served but to encircle himself with the image of lightning and the shores of his earth-race remained a sleeping door or blow of freedom.

Blow to freedom. I could not be sure in the pathology of space which was nearer the truth—blow to or blow of freedom. I began my investigations afresh by entering the seminal proportions of the staircase as if these were a new kind of "go-between"—a kind of waiting room or message which I planted and shared with the elders of land and water in and on whom I stood half-reflected, half-unreflected. As much as to say that only thus could I genuinely intercept that blow as coming from one end or arising from another on the globe, and rob it thereby of inflicting the fruit of fate (stoical child of the dead)—rope or snake that bit me on Matope.

So intercept the blow that my age—the age of the dead—would perceive its dual arrest, would *see* its greybeard institutions, helpless birthdays, year after year, century after century within the contusions of space as an intercessional wound between the unflinching child of god and the ancient scars of men.

Would see my age—the age of the dead—growing

out of its prison of arrest—deed of arrest—in such a way as to become the inconspicuous seed of waking sleep (Awakaipu's sleep) which had taken a century and more to begin to sprout through red pebble, green pebble, cured vision. I stood now within the seminal tree of Matope. An elder socket of water—an elder ghost of land—fertilized its own rain of elements like a bunched grape. It was this contradictory wound—pearl of heaven —that drew me to trace abrasion or eye reflected in fallow blood as it began to sprout. So that since one eye had aged a hundred years at least since Awakaipu's bruise into Awakaipu's grape, and the other hung heavy now upon its vine of space, it was the scale of the seed that branched through my dreams as the cured gorgon of heaven (pearl beyond price falling out of my head) into a lengthening age or shadow of vision that released the fatality of the universe from an unconscious snake upon god's wrist into Awakaipu's tree of Adam.

THE CURED GORGON OF HEAVEN

It was as if—standing now outside of Awakaipu's tear diversified by the gorgon of heaven into the wealth of space—I was aware of my own primitive seed that had aged without consciousness into its own cure of memory's bite—snake of the mind. Thus it was I was able to sprout all unseeing, still seeing, remembering nothing, remembering everything through the dead pupils of the earth-race shaped by the medicine-man as he spat on the globe—self-bite, self-anguish, self-reflecting humour or gland.

I knew I had come to the strangest bitten intersection in the staircase of dreams—unfeeling anguish of rain as it poured from his side or lips or eyes as from the gargoyle of creation (architecture of Awakaipu). It was here that the fountain of space shone on one hand as the dry-eyed paradox of heaven in the city of god—red and green traffic signals—sunrise and sunset bridegroom of souls, and faded on the other hand into a body of darkness.

For such a body may well have been the original fountain in the gorge of Awakaipu—without cure or injury, traffic of substitutes, lust or marble, visionary excreta. If therefore it had seemed in a flash (that pearl or tear falling from my head) to be memory's self-bite, drought and remorse (food of the gorgon) now it darkened equally into a time prior to the glands or humours of cruel ecstasy: into a sponge for which it could be mistaken as the greedy primitive sex of god. Seminal tragedy.

As it darkened it was as if its dripping feet had been set on a path away from every hill of execution, staircase or hall or room, cross or axe, sorrow of freedom, incestuous bullet. It was this seminal sponge of ages (prior to glands or humours or awakening blood) which sipped the tears of Awakaipu afresh on Matope as a hot and scalding landslide that seemed all the more crushing because it was bottomless, peerless, sponge of annunciation—all the more devastatingly intimate because it was tangential to an art of greed—gorge of soul.

I was drawn now to follow on the trail of the sponge as upon the long-lost path I had glimpsed of the age of the rainmakers. Its dripping feet seemed both consistent and inconsistent with the age of love—the age of showers beyond sea and land.

Consistent in that its departure from every chamber of sleep or simulated execution seemed to imply features of absorption—fountain of space—fountain of compassion—like a translating agency of biter and bitten, eyelid or bait of stars, wrinkle of heaven. As such it endorsed something prior to the fluid of man or the teeth of the devil—something in itself perfect (incapable of flaw or blemish) but endlessly appearing flawed, swollen and receptive, endlessly condensing the moisture of tragedy into a new precipitation of relief, new seed, new birth.

Inconsistent however in that the contents it harnessed in this way—moist galactic feet in suspension of the dance of death—seemed to bind the trail back to a film of need (chamber of earth). And the question arose— "Did the sponge of space squeeze its own blood in appearing to drink and redress the rivers of the dead?"

It was a question of ultimate fluid responsibility which began to reverberate like thunder across the landslide of age as I contemplated the massacre attributed to me by my German ghost or employer (mediumistic river of souls)—the hand of Awakaipu—"awakener of drought".

As though it was I whose primitive archetype of fire squeezed dry the colours of pity until not a bead remained, not a green star or tear, not a red drop of blood. Nothing but rags of drought—rags of cloud like tattered races or resurrections across the centuries through which

I felt as one who began to drown within generations of ambition in the antithesis of the sponge. Rags of drought. Fire-races of technology. Cloud-races of industry. I could feel the prophetic monolith of inhumanity (white painted black, black painted white) in my dead bones—the bridegroom of thunder—and I knew that the evaporation of colour in the lightning heart of the sponge had set its forge on Matope as though to brand me afresh with my own art or block, paint or canvas.

It was this paint of fire, paint of ultimate ironic responsibility, that served to blaze through me now the question of the wound of the sun—colour of bone—I had simulated as the seal of god on the face of my people. Yet he (the medicine-man of space) could harness his flood of compassion from my drought and remorse like a miracle of antithesis—like a river of *caveats* in a desert —like the sponge or age of newborn host as I relinquished my race of heaven to the rain of nativity.

The Laughter of the Wapishanas

NOTE

In 1948—when surveying in the upper Potaro Kaieteuran area of Guiana—I came upon a group of Wapishanas who are reputed to be a "laughter-loving" people unlike the fatalistically inclined Macusis and Arekunas.

The Wapishanas are neighbours of the Macusis and though they are said to be different in temperament they possess equally a certain decorum or ritual stiffness akin to a decoy of fate. At the time I remember making notes on the theme of laughter as the decoy of fate or vice versa.

Events within the past decade bear out the necessity for an imaginative relativizing agency within neighbouring though separate peoples whose promise lies in gateway conceptions of community.

The predicament of the Indian continues to deepen with new uncertainties as to the authority which governs him. Such authority has been at stake for centuries within the decimation of the tribes. And a political scale is still lacking: the land under his feet is disputed by economic interests and national interests. It is within this background that the theme of the decoy seems to me pertinent to the whole continent of South America. For not only does it reflect the ruses of imperialism which make game of men's lives but occupies a curious ground

61

of primitive oracle as well, whose horizons of sensibility we may need at this time to unravel within ourselves as an original creation.

Sermon of the Leaf

Somewhere on the staircase of the earth-race laughter was born in the sermon of the leaf. It was a curious inexplicable birth because there were years of drought when the source of laughter itself appeared to wither on the lips of the Wapishanas. A young girl of the tribe (herself called Wapishana) dreamt one day that she now cradled the dry mourning leaf of the elder tree of laughter.

She set out with it on the staircase of drought in search of the colour and nature of laughter—the source of laughter—which she was determined to restore to the lips of her people.

It was an ancient staircase which at that moment looked as dry and brown and wooden as the mourning leaf of the elder tree of laughter. It even had branches that seemed to issue in all directions as though to simulate the age of Wapishana's people: one branch for the elder tree of bird perched faraway in the dazzling reaches of the sky, one branch for the elder tree of fish swimming faraway in the dazzling bed of sky, one branch for the elder tree of animal concealed within bird and fish, one branch for the elder tree of god. . . .

These, amongst many other branches, seemed to

quiver almost as if they knew intimately the leaf of mission Wapishana bore as she knew her own tongue against her teeth. As if to whisper (one breath to another breathlessness, one flesh to another cage or prison) that that leaf she now carried in her head, in the markings of each palm or hand, sole or foot, had sprung from them —the walking tree or limbs of laughter—in the beginning of age when the people of Wapishana came along the elder branches of fate—along the branches of hunted bird and fish, animal and god.

Wapishana held their flesh or leaf, stamped irresistibly into the root of her senses, to her lips afresh and blew along its stiff razor-like edge as if to share something of the mingling of the sharpest blow of sorrow in the strings of laughter. It was as if the withered sliced lips of her people had become the sculpture of a song—an ancient feast of the bone which sometimes turned the tables of the tree on hunter by hunted in order to memorialize a silent debt of creation—creature to creature.

Wapishana decided to take the first leg of her journey back to the source of laughter along the elder tree of bird which stretched faraway into the dazzling reaches of the sky.

ELDER TREE OF BIRD

As Wapishana made her way along this limb of the tribe she felt herself betrothed in a curious way to the spirit of the wood: puberty of the tree.

At a certain juncture her ankles and wrists seemed

part of that branch—as if someone or something had grafted her there or sculpted her there into the tree of dreams: as if her thighs and breasts had been carved into a single memorial column with a knob where her forehead arched into bridge and nostrils, a crack where her lips stood from which a pointed leaf grew, tip of her tongue. It seemed almost derisory (that tip of her tongue)—tip of laughter at her own address, swaddling clothes, captive limb, bride of place.

As if the hunt of feathered species began with a joint or pact—elder bridegroom and derisory maiden—he (the elder tree) decked out with the yellow knob or beaked flame of the powis of the sun to woo her pointed sceptical leaf as a foretaste of humour—humour of bird-in-man, man-in-bird, reciprocal tongue of the psyche, marriage feast or memorial tree. She could not help laughing again at the grand air the bush turkey wore as self-sufficient decoy (powis and god, feathered man) as he approached her in solemn stiffness across or within the bough of fate. She continued to make a rude face at him—a mocking face at god—as he stiffly addressed her; and the leaf she bore which sprang from his feather became razor-sharp in their joint quarrel.

This leg of her journey towards the source of laughter had reached its first memorial juice of the skeleton—bridal feather-in-leaf whose pliant quarrel drew her to taste afresh an inexplicable humour of self-mockery in self-creation—vinegar of love. She felt it now on her lips (god's kiss)—kiss of sun upon maiden of drought like acid rainfall of secrets in mourning leaf or plant, blood in stone.

Wapishana recalled the morning she set out with the sun on her lips like a silent yellow beak shorn of its crest and wings. She recalled how she seemed part and parcel of the torn fabric of space—as if she herself were the scissors of fate which constituted her horizons. So that she moved and still did not move as though her scissors and legs—inner and outer horizons—permitted her to cut the cloth of heaven into progressive and variegated shapes. As if—in addition to the sun or shorn yellow beak on her lips—the leaf or word of the dance she bore in her head had been sliced into the palm of her hand, sole of her foot, crown of her head. Each step she made therefore corresponded to inner and outer crenelations of psyche—horizons of re-entry into the movement of creation akin to an approach to the universal mate of heaven. And each landmark she gained was less a question of marching time than of alterations of horizon—legs or scissors into decoy of space or reality of the game.

The apparition of the decoy signified unsmiling summons to the elder tree of fire. The apparition of the reality of the game signified smiling advance into the elder cloud of rain. And so the two were complementary like a comedy of passion wherein—on one circle or horizon—the yellow beak, crest, claws, feathers seemed to hover as one burning creature. On another the yellow beak, crest, claws, feathers broke—each at a tangent to the other—into separate items of dew in the morning mist.

The nature of this complement (as though nature wooed nature, night day) between fire and water became the ripple of laughter within the fold of the elements—cloth or flesh or wood. She recalled the mixed brew of scorn and pity that made her laugh at herself as a trophy of marriage—a smooth column with a knob for a forehead as the defiant leaf of her tongue smote him (mate of heaven) to the tune of broken address—knob on a stick—gleaming head of maiden-phallus. Thus Wapishana felt herself to be in the shining dew of god.

It was a curious way to become conscious of the smooth breach of herself through another whose fluid stroke was akin to her own brow jointed upon phallus (her trophy of penetration) so intermingled as to appear both the head of another, strange to herself, and the head of one, born of herself.

Wapishana had now travelled far back or through the ritual scissors (horizons) of the tribe—the age of puberty. It was an uncanny decoy upon which she sailed and the limbs she once possessed—holy and perfect—were turning inwards and outwards into a counter-revelation of parts that abolished the naked unselfconscious unity of the tribe. That dying unity—almost unrecognizable now as a communal mirror—served as a riddle of parts —numb comedy of man—divided source of laughter; for as Wapishana stood now on the threshold of the sliced mate of god—as she drew herself up to fly on the elder tree of bird—to spring through the open scissors of light she was aware, all at once, that something analogous had happened to her and the tribe a long time ago. Something in the nature of the leap she now wished to make. Something which had flown already from the other side of heaven through the horizons of age into her winged scissors. And as it leapt or flew then the horizons had closed—snapped shut upon her and upon it.

In closing, however, those scissors had fashioned her and saved her within the slice of memory from a timeless leap into total extinction—fashioned her and held her there (redress of death and life) to assemble a pall of rain as the gift of life.

ELDER TREE OF FISH

The second leg of her journey to the source of laughter took her along the elder tree of fish. A shower had fallen and the pool upon which Wapishana sailed was so clear she could see a cloud of fish like silver leaves in the hand of the sky. Each fish that she seized in turn settled in the palm of her hand as it fell from his (the hand of the sky) like a duplicate lifeline, duplicate sun in the water.

It was the strangest intercourse of fate—to be showered by this hand or mint—as before (upon the elder tree of bird) she had been kissed by the immanent beak of heaven and sliced by the immanent scissors of heaven.

Like a smiling, unsmiling merchant of fate—one hand wrinkling silver upon her—the other clawing gold about her—as he bargained for a style of death—plunge of the fish—maiden juice of extinction.

He had come a far way (the merchant of soul) in search of bait, scent, clue with which to beguile or redeem everything—annunciation of primitive lifeline. For this he was prepared to stake all he possessed upon an exotic *caveat* (pool of laughter).

Wapishana saw him (this merchant or bridegroom of conquest) approaching her upon the ritual staircase of god (decoy of reflection, decoy of pool) as the reification of everything—reification of juices of illusion: a reification within which one saw both the wealth and largesse of irony. It was this irony or *caveat* of nature she saw at the heart of the pool in which their reflected hands clasped, ironic lifeline of Christ, lifeline of the fish inscribed in her palm.

As with the horizons on the elder tree of bird—circle of unity on which the yellow beak, crest, claws, feathers of the sun seemed to hover as one creature—circle of dispossession on which the yellow beak, crest, claws, feathers advanced (each at a tangent to the other) like separate trophies of dew on branches of cloud—*so now* Wapishana was aware of horizons of depth akin to a lifeline of unity within her exotic grave, within the pool of wealth as the marriage portion of humanity—akin also to a landslide of greed within her exotic grave, within the rubble of wealth as wave of remorse.

So that as the merchant of soul held her (clasped her to his breast) he appeared to drown with her in all states of mankind, stone as well as flood, tyrannical or benign. To pull her down into the depths of the pool (draw her up again into every style of the paradox of death)—so that the very veil of the pool into which they plunged seemed to immure her, save her from (even as it seemed to immerse her, steep her in) extinction. Save her from death by drought as she stood within an original pall or cloud of rain.

ELDER TREE OF ANIMAL

As Wapishana made her way along the elder tree of animal she was aware of a buried arch or horizon now uplifted which had been concealed before within the elder tree of bird and elder tree of fish. It was an arch upon which, as she moved now, she became aware of sunrise at one end gradually piling up towards noon and apparently subsiding or filtering away as it descended towards the other end. And what was remarkable about this was that she began to perceive, for the first time, the progress of the tribe as a relative agent inclining to one absurd extreme or the other—absolute reification or absolute extinction. In fact that arch corresponded to a line that simulated the flight of a bird through the scissors of space or the lifeline of a fish from hand to hand upon which to measure the game of consciousness as one would collate the accumulated wisdom in the dispersal of the tribe through invitations issued by hunter to hunted—palm or summons of youth, crenellated fingers of age spread out across the sky, obverse or reverse decapitations or revolutions in the atmosphere.

Invitations which loomed on that arch as towering decoys of man looking towards sunset into which the game leapt (tall as a smouldering wall into the night): invitations which undermined those towers by looking towards sunrise across the pool of darkness into which the game leapt (inconspicuous as the seed of reality in the flare of a match).

At one end of the arch where the journey commenced

The Laughter of the Wapishanas

along the elder tree of animal Wapishana perceived the constellation of cloud known to the tribe as the golden age of laughter. It possessed many towers fashioned like claw and beak—wrinkled claw around the eyes of the tribe—wrinkled beak upon the lips of the tribe. There was a curious subsidence in that beak and claw buried in human flesh like gold in a giant's teeth (marsh of space). So that as Wapishana made her way through the golden age of laughter—half-sunken dawn, half-uplifted features—she felt the precariousness of her foothold, oscillations in cavern or mouth, anatomy of the feast.

Farther along the arch of the road—as Wapishana advanced and looked back—the head of the sun lay rusting now within its own mounds or mouthfuls of globe like the comedy of gold traced everywhere or the weight of laughter in bog or cosmos. And *flesh* had been engendered as this palimpsest of gold—fertility awakened as the miraculous soil of artifice. Each wrinkle or smile was the bed or track of beak and claw within the flesh of ancestor marsh or newborn swamp. Once again Wapishana was aware of every precarious leaf or foothold of sun in gigantic cities of cloud on the elder tree of animal as guarding against or being guarded by the subsidence of species.

Subsidence of species. Wapishana had the strangest sensation that every step she now took left her footprint in another's flesh so that the hardness of the globe became her self-deception akin to the merchant of soul—the decoy of soul—and the true game of reality (tender as the night) lay down the arch of the road *through* and *beyond* the purchase of extinction.

She now stood, however, somewhere in the middle of that arch (blocking the spirit of sunset) against the tower of noon, and behind her the golden age of laughter as it issued from the mouth of dawn or the rusting head of the sun seemed a kind of neolithic cloud—neolithic agriculture—comedy of the leaf. A leaf that still blew through the tower of noon like the flight of a bird or the dive of a fish until the path Wapishana took into the subjective precipitation of night seemed to echo to those footprints of beast in the thickness of air and thinness of water.

It was the thickness of air that constituted, in the first place, another's flesh of the beast in which she trod. It was the thinness of water, in the second place, that constituted another's flesh of the beast in which she trod from the beginning of time when man sold man to the elements. The tower of noon was the flesh of air. The tower of noon was the flesh of rain subtly conforming to Wapishana's footsteps in the moist places of earth as it steamed into dust or cloud equally susceptible again to the spoor of the tribe.

That spoor or footfall—in the subtlety or immateriality of tribal horizons—subsidence of globe—provided her with the first inklings of the decoy of night long before the tower of noon fell. In a sense the allure of night (the lair of the beast) had been measured for her in advance of her stride. And yet measureless it still was like a yielding substitute whose sponges were the graces of the void, the succulent mirror of god.

As she began to descend upon the sponge of air and water the reflection of noon seemed now less consistent with an absolute tower than with the sun's cap turned into a basin akin to the light footfall of space—lake in the sky—succulent mirror—lair of the fish.

And thus, slowly, increments of night were there long before night itself grew: invisible ruses of night in the crumbling dome of heaven: ruses akin to light veils— veil of lake upon fish—veil of chameleon—veil of spend-thrift gravity. It was the transparent decoy of night— aerial beast—at the heart of sunrise and sunset Wapishana followed through the towering redress of noon, veils of noon. That night had already fallen under the skin of day was the most contradictory vision of the lair of the beast that turned, as it were, its own primitive decoy of the dual senses into something far in advance of the onset of nature—prior to the onset of nature—a model of original extremity unfleshed by night or day.

ELDER TREE OF GOD

And thus Wapishana came through a veil that was no veil to stand on the last leg of her journey to the source of laughter—elder tree of god—cloud or model of original extremity unfleshed by night or day.

It stood there (that cloud) at the heart of antithesis— contradictory species of darkness—contradictory species of light. Wapishana attempted to grasp it as the assembly of yellow beak, crest, claws, feathers advancing into a single creature upon her—or departing, each at a tangent to the other, into the non-existent mate of heaven.

She attempted in the same token to visualize it as a

hollow shower or mint—maiden juice of extinction—comedy of the ironic bridegroom of the soul.

But however she looked at it it became senseless and faint except as the source of laughter—the first or the last model of man made in advance of the woman of the soil—in advance of bog or bed. As such it seemed to possess no authentic subsidence which could be verified —no sunrise, no sunset, no blood—but merely an unconscious plea that in its extremity it was the enduring laughter of the tribe which all would come to wear in death standing against drought—within another folded maiden light as veil or sap out of which the first stitch of rain would fall from the elder tree of god to tie a leaf to unfleshed wood.

Arawak Horizon

Sculpture is the mind of the skeleton.

Anonymous Epitaph

NOTE

Sven Loven in his Origins of the Tainan Culture, West Indies, *points out that* seme *is a true Arawak word akin to* zemi *which derives from the South American continent. In its manifestations within the Arawak consciousness* seme *or* zemi *appears to have a far-reaching sensitive role associated with poetry or sculpture which has been translated as "sweet" or "delicate".*

In some degree, I believe, "sweet" and "delicate" mirror a certain conception of frailty which makes all the more remarkable the survival of the Arawaks today in the Guianas when the fierce Caribs themselves who conquered them—long before Columbus came—have vanished in the twentieth century save for a remnant here and there.

In this story—the last in this volume—my intention is (as before) to concentrate on a personal exploration, within the late twentieth century, of vestiges of legend.

In defining this exploration as an arch or a horizon I have sought not to ring those vestiges round but to release them as part and parcel of the mind of history—the fertilization of compassion—the fertilization of the imagination—whose original unity can only be paradoxically fulfilled now through aspects of ruin or frailty within the material of consciousness through which one may begin to free oneself from overburden

79

and stress—*from fixtures and totalities—from conscriptions
and races—which may have been consolidated, in the first
place, as compensations of weakness.*

*It is in this new unshackled confessional sense, therefore, I
believe—on behalf of the Other whose past or future I inhabit
—that originality, coming from any source, fulfils the mind
of history by participating a seminal freedom or mathematic
of space arching through the prison of environment.*

One

─────────── ⟨❦⟩ ───────────

I dreamt I crossed the Arawak horizon at a point on the arch of space known as the mind of the skeleton where a giant sculpture rose out of ruined magma into sky-scraper day and night. Once upon a time it had been a total fire that could not be domesticated or swung away into the heavens like a great door or sun in space and it locked all men out (as tyranny of insulation) or in (as factor of extinction). Yet the key to that door fell into my hands long afterwards as I began to re-trace the undreamt-of steps of the prisoner of life through the Arawak sun. Undreamt-of, that is, until now as though I too had been fashioned by metamorphoses of volcano so that my dreams of reborn fire were his late passages of darkness, my eyes enslaved to light his corridors of gloom in the mountainside through the total fire of the sun into the original sculpture of night.

Mind of night in which intensities blazed at angles of vision to participate something of hollow cavity seminal to freedom, rooms or passages illuminated by conscious-ness to unfold a trail of numbers—dispersal of original fugitive or fugitives from the beginning of time—

O, I, 2, 3, 4, 5, 6, 7, 8, 9

articles or furnitures re-traced with a child's finger in ash or sand or dust as the code of the prisoner of life locked up in the Arawak sun.

Prisoner of the sun. Room of the sun. It was a distinction of originality that brought me up with a shock as I began to apprehend the hollow eyes of landscape— once both volcanic and unbearable, unapproachable—as the visionary numeral of life.

Who would have dreamt prior to the birth of night (soil or slate of stars) that a prisoner, or prisoners, had once stood there at the heart of fire to inscribe existences of freedom within a gaol of environment? To inscribe these with a pin of light comparable to a child's X-ray in the womb—X-ray finger invoking proportions, populations, dispersals upon the slate of darkness as the sun's body swung blind and open as night?

The first prisoner to creep through the walls of fire was inscribed by the child as ◯. ◯ had stood there, I dreamt, in my shoes (as I now in his or hers) within the ring of the furnace. Ring of fire which seemed to clasp him then to the breast of non-existence as it clasped me now through ash or dust, slate of numbers, soil of conception upon which to inscribe the origin of flight.

◯ was the child's first sculpture—mind of the skeleton. ◯ had been drawn or carved in the dust of the skyscraper like a window or bowl scooped out to signify no one and nothing and yet to suggest ironically that this record in itself—this style of vacancy—em-

bodied a sensibility across the ages through which to re-
create an arch—a journey backwards into the creation of
the Arawak sun. And that journey had begun when I
stumbled on to the slate of night upon which the child-
factor of god had been inscribed as an omen of fire.

Child-factor or ◯. It was as if I saw now the
seminal mathematic or key to the door of the sun. Door
and window. Bowl of subsistence. These were the instinctive properties of the ancient Arawak sun within
the newfound ash of place—palimpsest of stars created
by an original prisoner.

I began to look around carefully at the furniture in the
room of the Arawak sun, the bowl under the window,
the stars across the threshold in the wake of the door. I
knew I must acquaint myself intimately with this black/
white interior as the slate of memory and the chalk of
cosmos whose arch extended from primeval earth-
skeleton to modern skyscraper.

The prisoner I now embodied in the skeleton of the
mind had drawn a round face ◯ and beneath this a
stem to make ♀. I was conscious once again of the
sensibility of a key with which to unlock premises of
originality otherwise beyond dreams, beyond the link
of participation. My creation of the room of the Arawak
sun therefore possessed a stark almost undreamt-of sim-
plicity—a round head and a stem (◯ and |) that
metamorphosed itself into objects in the room as if these

were bound up in self-portraits of the prisoner. The key now turned into the skeleton of memory and became a table, a new item of furniture ♀ which revealed or unlocked itself within and upon the slate of night.

I lifted the bowl from the floor of the room and put it on the table and crouched before it like a man in prayer —subsistence of sun's grace. As I closed my eyes I began to embody an ancient dawning mathematic of darkened inwardness—a way of visualizing my folded limbs in the cosmos—whose first naïve Arawak inscription upon skyscraper looked like the kneeling figure of a star 2.

As I opened my eyes I was struck this time by the faceless bowl on the table like a bone in which some creature (myself) had gnawed a hole in the room of the Arawak sun. It was as if I supped now afresh on both remorse and compassion: compassion for a nameless animal I embodied and digested in the transubstantiation of numbers O, 1, 2 which invoked the life that endured through and in spite of the limits of deadly environment.

I recalled that when I had first seen the bowl on entering the room it had seemed to me part and parcel of a window. And now—as I concentrated upon it—still kneeling within the skyscraper sun—that aspect (the gnaw of space) returned, and I could see, through the window of the skeleton I dreamt I embodied, a strange and extinct beast innocent of cloud. It seemed to run within a non-atmosphere, within lifeless weatherless rainless sky, as if to invoke an impossible climate upon which my gaze was now bent (forwards into the future and backwards into the past) to reconstruct upon time and space a fantasia of extinct species.

"You see," I said to myself as to the musical ghost of time, "the paint of the sun serves as a primitive long-lost equation between an inhospitable ancient fire or sound and every barren newfound stretch of wilderness. As something akin to a splinter or crackle of bone in a room or desert. Nothing may live there except in our capacity to invoke that fragment as the food of memory arching across heaven like a rift in every static circumstance. We seek therefore, in salvaging an extinct species our ancestors pursued, to arouse afresh for future ages a conception of the game of weather on the deadliest planets situated beyond earth's atmosphere in the present like a fossil plateau situated within earth's dreaming crust in the past."

I gnawed at the bone in the Arawak sun and through the window of art depicting inhospitable space as relevant to the march of science sought to trace the slenderest backbone in the sky of the strange weathered beast of god I had thought extinct. In a sense it meant re-living the buried past arching through the present into the future as an evaporation of spirit signifying an existential rainbow or mnemonic waterfall.

Where the head and stem of the prisoner of the sun had appeared before two heads now stood—a head of spirit within a head of evaporation—slate of the sun—

circle within a circle ◉ rainbow within a rainbow.

But these soon readjusted themselves into a circle upon a circle making the figure 8 . Then 8 was sliced in half into a flattened half-circle upon a half-circle making self-portrait 3 . I turned this self-portrait of the rainbow on its bottom, arose from my knees and sat at the window like a cipher of fire ⍵ . A chair began to materialize beneath the prisoner (myself) within the desert of heaven—a high-backed chair which he (or I) drew with two strokes ∟ and then embodying the tension of circles and half-circles into a single line drew himself upright on his high-backed chair as the figure 4 .

It was curious but it was as if the glow of weather I sought to arouse through a waterless, primeval window had thrust its horns ⍵ into the prison of the Arawak sun as though to confirm the throned enigma of life. Would a maggot of rain spring from the anatomy of colours I embodied like a worm uncoiling itself for the first time in the drought of heaven? Or was this uncanny meat of rain—maggot of fertility—a witness of something apparently self-engendered but in reality *other* than premises of primeval corruption? Would the worm of rain come to signify something beyond its own atmosphere—something akin to a black star of life or ultra-violet slate?

These were the questions that had been unlocked by the subjective/objective key to the room of the sun. In the same way that I grew aware of horns of weather as my base of anatomy like a sliced **8 ω** turned on its curved bottom or side, so I was conscious now—as I sat at the window looking out as well as in—of the tail or brush of the cosmos plunging in the wake of its horns where my flesh was enthroned within the prisoner of constellations.

Two

————————❧————————

The tail of constellations—half-web, half-vacancy—
that swept the room was now an original blowing arch
that seemed to embody bowl ∪ and chair ∟ akin
to a portrait of the sun 5 (upside down shadowy
chair and sideways half-lit bowl). The wind sweeping
through the room turned the stars and articles within
into a fantasia of reconstruction like a musical score. The
prisoner himself who had long been freed as opus of fire
seemed now both rooted and aligned to bowl and chair
5 like anamnesis of a dance which stood him on his
head—arched back (bowl), bent knees, horizontal feet
(chair).

Thus it was the evaporation of spirit became the
genesis of freedom in furniture of arousal like self-
portraits of wind as if a great theme of flight were at the
heart of architectural motifs across the ages—architectural malaise—nostalgic periods, restoration of idols
—solipsistic tenancy.

The window of Arawak skyscraper at which I now
sat in the musical chair of the prisoner of old seemed

bent in the eye of a storm 6 like a curious maggot of vision or whirlpool or cycle of reflections blasting all complacency. It was the tail of fire uncoiling and coiling afresh around me into substitute existences or crumbling lights and walls of other existences (anamnesis of creation 7).

At first I wondered whether 7 was a child's copy or tracing of genesis (innocent re-statement of whirlpool sex or 6). 7 embodied a simple vertical stroke (prisoner's bar or body) drawn thus | and a simple horizontal beam or erection drawn thus —— which turned in all directions 7 or ⌐ . But on closer fiery reflection or deeper consideration of 6 (coil of space) and 7 (marriage to space) I was conscious of something non-derivative, non-naturalistic in the revolution of earth-skeleton into skyscraper—the tail of vanishing pre-history into the arousal of metamorphosis.

"What do you mean by non-naturalistic?" 7 and ⌐ said to me and (as wind and fire blew) they drew together into a joint signal like a child's star or the wing-span and thrust of an ambivalent flying machine in the Arawak unconscious ⋏ .

"By non-naturalistic," I said in order to humour 7

and Γ within a diaspora of elements ∧ , "I mean the breakthrough of original dimensions—seminal rediscovery (*zemi* or *seme*) rather than a derivative escape route into the past. I mean the living genesis of the cornerstone of time involving and revolving within the light of creation rather than cloaked in furnishings or ranks which imprison us as total models of the sun. I mean the signature of the original prisoner of life whose mathematic of otherness (death translating life, life death) is the *caveat* of freedom without which we are doomed to reproduce uniform environments of hate and to hanker after romantic 'green' substitutes we reinforce or bind into tautological nature—gaol or fortress."

7 and Γ were grimly laughing like the blackened limbs of the prisoner of old—*caveat* of fire—in halfway house to the cross or the tree ✝

"Creation", I continued, "is a non-derivative balance of resources and therefore it is involved in a breakthrough from a purely formal pattern (or deed of materialism) into a primitive/scientific cosmos beyond civilization's end-products (end-products of hate or punitive love)."

At last the full implications of my penetration of the Arawak sun (metamorphoses of the game of weather) were becoming clear. I was involved in the breakthrough of an original prisoner of life from metaphorical deadly furnace or total green nature (from insane

obsessional age or idealistic crime of youth). As though
—in order to distinguish between creations and models,
the law of spirit and the execution of the deed, genesis
and earth—I needed to experience a devolution of space
intrinsic to rooms of otherness: intrinsic to the music of
rain beyond the roof of the skies. The skyscraper of man
embodied a motif of evaporation pointing to the
drought of stars as to dry rain (unearthly ruin of space) in
advance of a ceiling of water or mask of heaven.

As such—in both ceiling and breakthrough—I was
involved in the flight of the prisoner of god (in his
vacant room or primitive dome) as in a new epic of the
elements beyond the worship of nature. I was involved
in the bowl of creation to which I turned now as to the
receptacle of the prisoner, dry rain (unearthly ruin) upon
which he supped—the seminal digestion of a bone of
water by the prisoner of god in advance of cloud or
model.

The gnawed bone or bowl of space stood on the table
of the Arawak skyscraper like this $\bigcup$. I was aware, as I
supped, of another bowl I had previously overlooked in
my inventory of the stars and furnitures in the room:
another bowl to imply there had been someone else to
bear the prisoner company or to suggest that even then
long, long ago he knew I would come and thus he
proffered me the core of his hospitality *in my absence* as I
supped now with him *in his*. Sitting there now I knew he
and I had been created in the beginning before I
materialized within his imagination of night or he de-
materialized within my imagination of day.

The proxy bowl of creation had been turned down on the table thus ∩ and on an impulse I raised it and placed it upon mine like this 8 to invoke the fire of rain from hollow to hollow by rubbing dry bones together. As I scraped and pressed rim to rim, receptacle to receptacle, the Arawak horizon was sealed into the conjunctive vision of the prisoner of god 8 eighth day of the spectacles of creation ∞ skeleton of rain and light of construction.

I felt now I was half-assembling, half-groping towards or into something related to an immense witness of an evaporation of spirit (flight of god) as I supped with the prisoner in the conjunctive horizons of a primitive/scientific cosmos. I put his spectacles on me like articulate inner/outer bones (seminal match or digestion of features) and the tail of the stars on the floor of the skyscraper suddenly threaded my eyes like the teeth of a saw—molars or millstones of god—visionary ground of consciousness within the jaw of the Arawak sun.

What sort of creation, self-made carpenter of life (my brain reeled at the flight of origins) had he been? His tail arched and still did not arch (web and vacancy): his jaw of stars traced (and still did not trace) the game of weather. His horns were the anatomy of music. Had he possessed visionary teeth (eye-teeth) of a kind of relative cutting splendour—the *saw* or mathematics of a family of suns? Had he made himself—in order to fall into himself—into the furnace of nature? Had he cut the doors of night (the black doors of space)—in order to fall out of himself—out of the furnace of nature?

And as he fell—had he framed the fire of revolutions —mother of light—mistress of darkness? "YES and NO," he replied over the rim of his bowl upon which was distilled a child's drawing of night and day as the roast of rain on which I supped—goddess of fertility;

planted her breasts and made her womb ஐ shaped

a triple *zemi* of cloud in the roof of the Arawak sun.

Thus began the curious feast of otherness—within-ness to without-ness—which characterized a fall into and out of the goddess he framed—conception of primitive reason—evaporation of primitive reason—match of seasons.

Tall and short were the teeth of the rain as earth-skeleton arched into skyscraper.

Three

First I clambered upon the tall teeth in the jaw of god as though I had changed places with the roasted rain and found myself in process of being eaten by another rather than in process of eating another. My window or environment as I climbed was barred like ivory; ivory rain. And I dreamt that these bars were a fertile prisonhouse (genes of penetrance) forked cruelty of god, match of nature like blue blood upon the ivory roof of the sun.

It was this sheen or illusion that imprinted itself upon me as a total mask of effects—blue dome, ivory jaw—a total capacity with which to rake the elements in the name of skyscraper clown, skyscraper colony, skyscraper superman, skyscraper underling. The tall teeth of environment supped upon me as if I had been designed the lowliest of creatures—roasted rain in the jaw of ivory rain: roasted sun in ivory sun. And this frame of subjective dominance became my first volcanic mirror, deadly romantic gaol or order of hierarchical crime, my first model illusion of the original body of creation. Arawak of the beanstalk. Tall Jack-tooth (Jackboot) of rain. On that arch or giant tooth—reaching up to indentations of appetite as well as down to the

94

spoor of the tribe—I waited for the jaw of god to close upon me, and as it did so the blue dome of illusion, the ivory footfall of the rain turned red as the underbelly of the sea—volcanic Arawak legend of the body of god through which the sun was on fire as it set.

It was my imagination of night that the throat of god became black like soot—black dome of earth instead of blue. As though my roasted rain—rain of my blood— had filled the mouth of god almost to overflowing. And swept me now into a deeper tide—footfall of gloom— that had spanned the sun. I could hear nevertheless, even as I thought I would be kicked up or cast down, the bars of weather clash shut behind me to frame the wind, to frame a breath on the fiery sea of space: bottle-neck heaven and hell.

Slowly, as I continued to climb up (or was it down?) genetic beanstalk or black tooth of the sun, I waited for the jaw of god to open again as it had closed upon me a little while ago. I wondered if, in opening, it would let me fall back into the bowl on the table upon which the prisoner supped. And if, in thus falling back—falling out of the pit of night into the pit of day—I would have discovered the origins of fertility, the inconspicuous origins of the goddess of fertility, as a strange reflective morsel held on the tongue of the pit against the teeth of the pit, then on the lips of the pit to moisten another's tongue, against another's teeth, upon another's lips. I would have discovered the very delicacy, the *zemi* of sweetness, the rarity of communication *through* the bars of the pit—the pit of environment.

Tall and short were the teeth of the rain as I dreamt of

myself in a reflective morsel, smouldering kiss of the pit (lips of famine to lips of plenty). First I remembered I had climbed the giant's tall tooth; now it seemed as I waited for the jaw to reopen I slid on to a stump. On this stump—traced by the tongue of the pit—I discerned within the grave of night what seemed to me the sculpture or footprint of a fallow deer ⋈ drought deer in the mouth of space.

I knew I must fly with it; spring with it; voyage from the tongue of the pit. So that in the giant kiss of night and day I would stumble upon as well as leap through the giant void. And in this inner/outer devouring trail of another complex of personality which I tasted, and through which I was tasted myself by the other, I began to *see* something of the evaporation of god, flying spirit-deer, spirit-rain, spirit-fire whose arch of space repudiated a total paradise as prejudicial to the wraith of man upon a trail of *caveats*—fallow tooth (footprint) of the ghost of oneself—a self one dreams as wholly consumed in the jawbone of gods/goddesses through which one leaps to scale freedom.

Four

———— ❦ ————

I dreamt I had discovered in my Arawak cosmos a
child's drawing 8 turned sideways into the drought
footprint of a deer ⠍. Spirit-deer, absent rain-deer
which re-shaped itself now into one remaining circle
and one open line or tangent ⊋ that later slid out
into the tail of the sun ⊋.

I began to grope afresh into the waif of god or ninth
day of the prisoner of life whose self-portrait I embodied
across the ages at the tail of the sun: dying race, flying
sun. As though I saw myself anew with distant single
eye, handle of premises, baton of relays within an
architecture of music or spine of rain. I saw myself far
back in the sound of space, in the jaw of space—circle
of peril where he (I) stood, poised to run.

That poise or threshold was the strangest expenditure
of himself like the pace of the wind or the stroke of a
wave to re-conceive me long afterward. It was his
breath of dancing consciousness prior to my self-
portrait of the birth of music, the sound of rain. I saw
him then as the inner paradox of myself—the very

97

breath or arousal of my elements. I could see a deep pool of reflection like a furnace as though he invoked my fearful contradiction: superior fury/inferior frame: man as the frame of god: water as the ring of fire, earth as the footstool of heaven.

"When he flew," I asked myself, "did he die to manifest me as his compensation of life, when he ran did he fall to provide me with contours of endurance, when he stood still did he grow unconscious to embalm my station of nature as his promissory note of god, covenant of god?"

The riddle of my self-portrait had barely flooded my senses when I saw what seemed to me compensatory witnesses or features of the evaporation of god, the ninth day of heaven.

First he had flown into the wind and in order to compensate his invisibility through me, the invisibility of the wind, had turned the objects in the room of the sun round and round into self-portraits of music, self-portraits of the falling themes of spiritual consciousness.

It was as if—prior to flying into the wind, prior to the creation of the invisible wind—he (I) stood at the door or window of the sun on the very edge of a precipice. Nothing moved since the wind had not yet simulated itself into my limbs as waif of man $\wedge$ or $\dagger$. Nothing moved until space became ivory as an antediluvian cloak in one light, grey stone or fossil goatskin in another light, blue-black wood or primitive painted canoe in still another light. Hard bleak fleet of appearances whether ivory or grey or black—as though space began to portray itself as the savage compensation of his death the instant he leaped and I was drawn. Drawn to the gravity of his theme through which the lights of space were assembled in me: drawn to the spirit of his motion through which the canoe of space enveloped me.

It was this gravity I entreated as it cloaked me now with his flight. There it was—cloak of gravity—skyscraper canoe or tower—glazed here, diamonded there with splinters from his abyss which stared at me; splintered address I was conscious of as something prior and open to my self-portrait of the wind—something in the nature of an economic capacity to witness of him when I blew across the walls of my skyscraper. And I knew that when I painted his flight, when I conceived myself falling and being crushed anew into a savage assembly of lights, *when I dreamt it was I who fell and died*, I saw through his abyss of gravity. I SAW THROUGH HIS ABYSS OF GRAVITY. One day that towering abyss or frozen savage skyscraper of god I drew as my self-portrait would fall in its turn and drift into another's consciousness or location of dead colour on the wall of the sun. One day it would stand watching him. The next it would fall watched by him. Thus a perspective or corridor of witnesses would extend beyond self-portrait of paradox to self-portrait of paradox like death witnessing to the colours of death or the subtlest breakthrough in the endless compositional rhythms of life.

That perspective was the theme of the wind (precession of architectures) in which objects became self-portraits of flight—towers became hollow shafts—

economic wings to an apparently falling theme of shared spiritual origins: thus did he (I) begin to visualize and create a body of wealth, the evolution of consciousness as bars of sound, impact of music, doors and windows of skyscraper canoe: superior flight/inferior frame in the opus of the incarnations of god.

I (he) flew into the architecture of music. He (I) created the painted sound of flesh and blood like a long train of infinite objects in whose prior native abyss I (he) dreamt it was spring, the spring of achievement.

FIRST THEREFORE HE (I) HAD FLOWN INTO THE SCULPTURE OF THE WIND. . . .

Second he ran into the heart of vision and in order to compensate the brightness of immateriality had turned the objects in the room into self-portraits of light—incandescent theme of spiritual consciousness which began to darken into milestones and monuments.

Thus—looking back at the furnace of the Arawak sun—I saw it now as one of his first black milestones or witnesses to a theme of vision threaded to the evaporation of fire, death of fire, rebirth of fire.

It was a hard economic monument to bear—to look back upon as I dreamt I sped with his winged feet into the night. He had run and died to all intents and purposes and the cold blaze of the sun in his wake seemed mournfully and blissfully unaware it had addressed him as bank or temperature before he ran and flew.

It dawned on me now that the first black door to open in a poem of fire was a spark of recognition in the colours of the blind—blind fire to blind water—black priority to blazing priority—like the death of fire dislodging itself from every monument into a runway of vision. THUS IT WAS IN THE SECOND PLACE HE SURRENDERED HIMSELF TO THE THEME OF LIGHT AS MANIFESTED IN THE IMPACT OF FURIES, HOT AND COLD GIANT KISS OF SELF-PORTRAITS OF ATTRITION ON THE WHEELS OF NIGHT AND DAY, GAIN AND LOSS, BLACK AND WHITE GHOST OF OCEANIC PREMISES.

In the third place he grew still and in order to compensate a loss of movement, or unconsciousness of movement, he embalmed the drought of nature as the promissory note or covenant of god, economics of rivers, evaporation or impending cosmic fall.

Thus—looking back like the ghostly composer/painter/rainmaker of contours of the void—I saw him as my besieged ironical tower, manifestation or bank of premises. Like someone conscripted by the gorgon of the sun—someone whose steady weight served as the most alien shore or extremity of love at the heart of my gentlest oceanic folk. Milestone of Arawak survival across the seas of soul.

It was a bitter economic lighthouse to bear—that once a furnace of environment like the icy grip of hell had invested the prisoner of life. And that it seemed feasible to dream no one or nothing could have lived there at all, neither within in the heat nor without in the cold of such a whirlpool of ice or fire, save a far-flung spark of consciousness which intimated—in that breakthrough from no one and nothing (ice and fire)—that the survival of anyone and anything, after all, upon the earth was explicable in paradoxes or self-portraits of spiritual themes. The self-portraits of the invisible wind—theme of frosted music, glittering hail or sparks of dew—were dancing objects or furnitures in space. The self-portrait of immaterial light—theme of vision—was an ironic salutation of the blind colour of sun to the blind colour of water in preserving as well as energizing an explosion of consciousness. The self-portrait of mathematics— theme of absent numbers—was an ultra-violet slate of stars. So, too, in the embalmed fortunes of nature lay the theme of ironic perfection—freedom's fortress of perfection and immortality as an evaporation of spirit signifying someone beyond a circumstantial bier or antithesis of breath witnessing to every vanished life.

I looked back as I ran and flew with a sense of curious awe at the embalmed breathless vistas of earth as models of ironic perfection. In the glaze of distance those vistas may have been parchment of fire or parchment of flood. As parchment of fire earth seemed a perfect dead seal on all things. As parchment of flood earth seemed equally perfect, equally sealed or model of deadly environment. But now I perceived in that glaze of primeval distances the irony of god implicit in the flight of the prisoner: I perceived myself as an interface of elements which was both the antithesis of the seal of fire or water as well as the ceaseless mystery or breakthrough of creation into consciousness. A breakthrough which seemed in some ways the comedy of creation—antithesis of the economics of stasis, antithesis of the stasis of immortality.

I looked back as I ran and flew at the stasis of immortality (frame of god) as my most macabre outpost of the imagination where the art of self-sufficiency was so entrenched (embalmed fire or embalmed flood) that it glistened with an unconscious opposite apparition like the glazed eye of water searching for fire or the glazed eye of fire searching for water, breathlessness searching for breath. It was this glaze which now became the soul or mirror of space witnessing for the themes of the prisoner of creation in the room of the Arawak sun.

I looked forward now as I ran and flew, with the sense that in visualizing these mirrors ∞ (spectacle of fire, spectacle of water) as self-portraits of breath allied to breathlessness, I was involved in the curious reversal of the stasis of immortality into winds of fortune. As a consequence the economics of immortality, which was earth, turned round and round as my self-portrait, fortunate music, wealth of comedy I inherited from space as an upside down chair and sideways laughing bowl 5 acrobatic water.

The sun also turned round and round as my self-portrait or fortunate paint, acrobatic fire, whose arch was the wealth of divinity I inherited from space, tail of my Arawak cosmos 9 signposting the spine of the wind in the stars—treasury of The Rainmaker.

As he (The Rainmaker) ran and flew—looked back, looked forward—he was aware of himself as signifying losses therefore embodying gains in a self-portrait of the currency of time; signifying a fall therefore embodying a rise in the self-portrait of the hill of time; signifying invisible themes therefore embodying a visible frame or self-portrait of the comedy of time; signifying an evaporation of spirit therefore embodying a precipitation of life as winds of fortune blowing on every horizon or wilderness of suns.